Let's Pretend

written by Gina Gold
illustrated by Tom Brannon

Reader's Digest
Children's Books®

New York, New York • Montréal, Québec • Bath, United Kingdom

Ahoy, Matey!

"I love to splish and splash in the pool," squealed Zoe with delight.

Elmo laughed and swooshed his toy boat through the water. "Zoe, what do you think it would be like to be a pirate in a giant ship?" he asked.

"If I were a pirate," Zoe said excitedly, "I'd live on a desert island and eat coconuts for breakfast, lunch, and dinner!"

"Land ho! I see you, Zoe!" giggled Elmo.

Let Down Your Hair!

"Look! Elmo is a superhero!" said Elmo, as he and his friends played dress up. "Next, Elmo will be a fireman and then a race car driver!"

"I'd like to be a princess living in a tall tower," said Zoe. "And I'd wait for a knight to come and rescue me."

"Elmo could be a knight, but how would Elmo rescue you?" Elmo asked.

"You would just say, 'Fair Zoe, lovely Zoe, pretty Zoe...let down your hair!'" Zoe answered.

"Fairy tales are so enchanting," giggled Abby. "I would ride a friendly dragon and visit castles in the clouds."

Left, Right, Left, Right, March!

"Elmo, listen to that wonderful music," said Zoe. "I would love to play the saxophone."

"Oh, that sounds fun, Zoe!" agreed Elmo. "Someday we could all play instruments and be in the Sesame Street marching band!"

"What instrument would you play, Grover?" asked Zoe.

"I would play the very sweet little flute," said Grover.

"Oh, I'd play the sassy saxophone," dreamed Zoe. "I like the way it sounds."

"Everyone would make beautiful music together," chimed in Elmo.

Time to Climb...a Mountain!

Whoosh! "Hold on, Cookie!" Zoe called out as her sled flew down the hill.

"Here comes Elmoooooo!" shouted Elmo as he passed them.

At the bottom of the hill, Zoe cried out, "Let's do it again!"

"Let's pretend we're mountain climbers," said Elmo, as he trudged through the snow. "We'll be the first to make it to the top of the tallest mountains in the world!"

"I will plant a flag at the tippy-top!" said Zoe, triumphantly. "*Oooo.* This mountain is so high I can see Sesame Street far, far away!"

Dinosaur Days

"*Grrr, Grrrr,*" said Elmo, as he and Zoe played with toy dinosaurs. "Elmo wishes Elmo could see a real dinosaur!"

"Me, too," said Zoe. "There are so many different dinosaurs to learn about! It's too bad dinosaurs lived a very, very long time ago."

"If Elmo could meet one dinosaur, it would be the Apatosaurus. It was BIG," Elmo said as he made his toy dinosaur stomp and roar.

"I'd like to slide down their long necks!" said Zoe, giggling. "I wish we had some real dinosaur friends today. They'd be the biggest pals on the playground!"

Farming Is Fun!

"Spring is here! Let's plant tomatoes, carrots, lettuce, and squash in the community garden," Murray said.

"*Squaaaash!* Elmo likes how that sounds," said Elmo. "Elmo can't wait for these vegetables to grow. If Elmo were a real farmer, Elmo would have a big red barn and tractor."

"I'd have animals like sheep and cows to take care of," said Zoe. "I'd feed and talk to them every day."

"I would like growing vegetables best," said Murray. "When they are ripe, I would pick them and make a healthy salad to gobble up!"

All Aboard!

"I love to travel to faraway places," said Zoe.

"Elmo does, too," said Elmo. "Elmo wants to travel across America on a great big locomotive!" he added. "Let's line up our chairs and take turns pretending we're train conductors!"

"All aboard!" Zoe cried out. "The train is leaving! First stop is Sesame Street!"

"Pull the train whistle, Zoe! *Whoo, whoo!*" Elmo shouted.

With the Greatest of Ease

"*Wheeee!*" said Zoe, swinging through the air. "Pump, Elmo, pump!"

"Watch Elmo stretch to reach the sky!" Elmo called to his friend. "Elmo thinks this is what it feels like to be a trapeze artist at the circus!"

"If I were a trapeze artist, I would do flips and twirl through the air," Zoe answered.

"Hooray for Zoe!" Elmo said excitedly. "When you are done doing tricks, it's time to take a bow while everyone claps and cheers!"

Roughing It

"Camping in your house is the best kind of sleepover there is," Zoe told Elmo. "It's always perfect weather and there are always yummy snacks."

"In a tent," said Elmo, "Elmo and Elmo's friends can pretend to be anywhere in the world."

"If I were really camping, I'd like to be in the Grand Canyon," Zoe said excitedly.

"The Grand Canyon is great for hearing your voice echo. Like this: *Elmo-O-O-O-O!*"

"We could also toast yummy cookie over campfire," added Cookie Monster.

Zoom to the Moon

"Look at all those sparkly stars!" said Elmo. "There are so many!"

"And there's the moon!" said Zoe. "I can see a face in it!"

"Elmo wishes Zoe and Elmo could fly to the moon," said Elmo.

"We could if we pretend to be astronauts," said Zoe.

"Elmo wants to ride a rocket to the moon right now. Blast off!" said Elmo. "It's fun to imagine."